Anonymous

The Army Hymn-Book

Anonymous

The Army Hymn-Book

ISBN/EAN: 9783337083434

Printed in Europe, USA, Canada, Australia, Japan

Cover: Foto ©Andreas Hilbeck / pixelio.de

More available books at **www.hansebooks.com**

THE

ARMY

HYMN-BOOK.

RICHMOND VA:
PRESBYTERIAN COMMITTEE OF PUBLICATION.
1863.

HYMNS.

WORSHIP.

C. M.

APPROACH my soul, the mercy-seat,
  Where Jesus answers prayer,
There hum'ly fall before his feet,
  For none can perish there.

Thy promise is my only plea,
  With this I venture nigh;
Thou callest burden'd souls to thee,
  And such, O Lord, am I.

Bow'd down beneath a load of sin,
  By Satan sorely press'd,
By war without, and fear within,
  I come to thee for rest.

Be thou my shield and hiding place;
  That shelter'd near thy side,
I may my fierce accuser face,
  And tell him "thou hast died."

Oh! wond'rous love, to bleed and die,
  To bear the cross and shame,
That guilty sinners, such as I,
  Might plead thy gracious name.

5   C. M.

BLESS'D be the everlasting God,
    The Father of our Lord ;
Be his abounding mercy praised,
    His majesty adored.

2 When from the dead He raised his Son,
    And called Him to the sky,
He gave our souls a lively hope,
    That they should never die.

3 What though our inb'ed sins require
    Our flesh to see the dust ;
Yet as the Lord our Saviour rose,
    So all his followers must.

4 There's an inheritance divine,
    Reserved against that day ;
'Tis uncorrupted, undefiled,
    And cannot fade away.

Saints by the power of God are kept,
    Till that salvation come ;
We walk by faith as strangers here,
    Till Christ shall call us home.

6   H. M.

BLOW ye the trumpet, blow;
    The gladly solemn sound,
Let all the nations know,

To earth's remotest bound,
The year of jubilee is come;
Return, ye ransom'd sinners, home

2 Jesus, our great High Priest,
  Hath full atonement made;
Ye weary spirits, rest; .
  Ye mournful souls, be glad;
The year of jubilee is come:
Return, ye ransom'd sinners, home

3 Exalt the Lamb of God,
  The sin-atoning Lamb;
Redemption in his blood
  To all the world proclaim:
The year of jubilee is come;
Return, ye ransom'd sinners, home.

4 Ye slaves of sin and hell,
  Your liberty receive,
And safe in Jesus dwell,
  And bless'd in Jesus live;
The year of jubilee is come;
Return, ye ransom'd sinners, home.

5 Ye who have sold for naught
  Your heritage above,
Receive it back unbought,
  The gift of Jesus' love; .
The year of jubilee is come;
Return, ye ransom'd sinners, home.

6 The gospel trumpet sounds,
  Let all the nations hear,

And earth's remotest bounds,
 Before the throne appear ;
The year of jubilee is come ;
Return, ye ransom'd sinners, home.

7   7 s.

COME, my soul, thy suit prepare,
 Jesus loves to answer prayer ;
He himself has bid thee pray,
Therefore will not say thee nay.

2 With my burden I begin,
Lord, remove this load of sin ;
Let thy blood, for sinners spilt,
Set my conscience free from guilt.

3 While I am a pilgrim here,
Let thy love my spirit cheer ;
As my Guide, my Guard, my Friend,
Lead me to my journey's end.

4 Show me what I have to do,
Every hour my strength renew ;
Let me live a life of faith,
Let me die thy people's death.

8   C. M.

COME, let us join our cheerful songs,
 With angels round the throne ;
Ten thousand thousand are their tongues,
 But all their joys are one.

2 "Worthy the Lamb that died," they cry,
    "To be exalted thus."
"Worthy the Lamb," our lips reply,
    "For He was slain for us."

3 Jesus is worthy to receive
    Honor and power divine;
And blessings more than we can give,
    Be, Lord, for ever thine.

4 Let all that dwell above the sky,
    And air, and earth, and seas,
Conspire to lift thy glories high,
    And speak thine endless praise.

5 The whole creation join in one
    To bless the sacred name
Of Him that sits upon the throne,
    And to adore the Lamb.

9   8 s & 7 s.

COME, thou Fount of every blessing,
    Tune my heart to sing thy grace:
Streams of mercy, never ceasing,
    Call for songs of loudest praise.
Teach me some melodious sonnet,
    Sung by flaming tongues above;
Praise the mou t; O fix me on it,
    Mount of God's unchanging love.

2 Oh, to grace how great a debtor
    Daily I'm constrained to be!

Let that grace, Lord, like a fetter,
  Bind my wandering heart to Thee.
Prone to wander, Lord, I feel it;
  Prone to leave the God I love:
Here's my heart, Lord, take and seal it,
  Seal it for thy courts above.

10   C. M.

FATHER of mercies, in thy word
  What endless glory shines!
For ever be thy name adored,
  For these celestial lines.

2 Here may the wretched sons of want
  Exhaustless riches find;
Riches, above what earth can grant,
  And lasting as the mind.

3 Here the Redeemer's welcome voice,
  Spreads heavenly peace around;
And life and everlasting joys
  Attend the blissful sound.

4 O may these heavenly pages be
  My ever dear delight;
And still new beauties may I see,
  And still increasing light.

5 Divine instructer, gracious Lord,
  Be thou for ever near;
Teach me to love thy sacred word,
  And view my Saviour there.

11   7 s,

LORD we come before thee now,
    At thy feet we humbly bow;
O do not our suit disdain;
Shall we seek thee, Lord, in vain?

2 Lord, on thee our souls depend;
In compassion, now descend;
Fill our hearts with thy rich grace;
Tune our lips to sing thy praise.

I In thine own appointed way,
Now we seek thee, here we stay;
Lord, we know not how to go,
Till a blessing thou bestow.

I Send some message from thy word,
That may joy and peace afford;
Let thy spirit now impart,
Full salvation to each heart.

I Comfort those who weep and mourn,
Let the time of joy return;
Those who are cast down, lift up,
Make them strong in faith and hope.

I Grant that all may seek and find
Thee a God supremely kind:
Heal the sick, the captive free;
Let us all rejoice in thee.

12 L. C. M.

WHEN thou, my righteous Judge, shalt com
 To take thy ransomed people home,
 Shall I among them stand?
Shall such a worthless worm as I,
Who sometimes am afraid to die,
 Be found at thy right hand?

2 I love to meet among them now,
Before thy gracious feet to bow,
 Though vilest of them all;
But can I bear the piercing thought,
What if my name should be left out,
 When thou for them shalt call?

3 Prevent, prevent it by thy grace,
Be thou, dear Lord, my hiding place,
 In this the accepted day;
Thy pardoning voice, O let me hear,
 To still my unbelieving fear,
 Nor let me fall, I pray.

4 Let me among thy saints be found,
Whene'er the archango's trump shall sound,
 To see thy smiling face;
Then loudest of the crowd I'll sing,
While heaven's resounding mansions ring,
 With shouts of sovereign grace.

13 L. M.

WHAT various hindrances we meet,
 In coming to a mercy-seat!

Yet who that knows the worth of prayer,
But wishes to be often there?

2 Prayer makes the darkened cloud withdraw,
Prayer climbs the ladder Jacob saw,
Gives exercise to faith and love,
Brings every blessing from above.

3 Restraining prayer, we cease to fight;
Prayer makes the Christian's armor bright;
And Satan trembles when ho sees
The weakest saint upon his knees.

4 Have you no words? Ah! think again,
Words flow apace when you complain,
And fill your fellow-creature's ear,
With the sad tale of all your care.

5 Were half the breath thus vainly spent,
To heaven in supplication sent,
Your cheerful song would oftener be,
"Hear what the Lord has done for me."

THE SAVIOUR.

14   C. M.

ALAS and did my Saviour bleed,
    And did my Sovereign die!
Would He devote that sacred head.
    For such a worm as I?

2 Thy body slain, dear Jesus, thine,
    And bathed in its own blood;
  While all exposed to wrath divine,
    The g'orious sufferer stood.

3 Was it for crimes that I had done,
    He groaned upon the tree?
  Amazing pity! grace unknown!
    And love beyond degree!

4 Well might the sun in darkness hide,
    And shut his glories in,
  When God, the mighty Maker, died,
    For man, the creature's sin.

5 Thus might I hide my blushing face,
    While his dear cross appears;
  Dissolve my heart in thankfulness,
    And melt my eyes to tears.

6 But drops of grief can ne'er repay
    The debt of love I owe:
  Here, Lord, I give myself away;
    'Tis all that I can do.

15   C. M.

ALL hail the power of Jesus' name!
    Let angels prostrate fall;
  Bring forth the royal diadem,
    And crown Him Lord of all.

2 Ye chosen seed of Israel's race,
   Ye ransomed from the fall ;
   Hail Him, who saves you by his grace,
   And crown Him Lord of all,

3 Sinners, whose love can ne'er forget
   The wormwood and the gall ;
   Go, spread your trophies at his feet,
   And crown Him Lord of all.

4 Let every kindred, every tribe,
   On this terrestrial ball,
   To Him all majesy ascribe,
   And crown Him Lord of all.

5 O that with yonder sacred throng,
   We at His feet may fall ;
   We'll join the everlasting song,
   And crown Him Lord of all.

16   8 s, 7 s & 4 s.

HARK ! the voice of love and mercy
   Sounds aloud from Calvary ;
See ! it rends the rocks asunder,
   Shakes the earth and veils the sky.
      "It is finish'd !"
   Hear the dying Saviour cry.

2 It is finish'd !—Oh, what pleasure
   Do the wondrous words afford !
Heavenly blessings without measure,

Flow to us through Christ the Lord.
　　It is finish'd !
Saints, the dying words record.

3 Tune your harps anew, ye seraphs;
　　Strike them to Immanuel's name:
All on earth and all in heaven,
　　Join the triumph to proclaim,
　　　　It is finish'd !
　　Glory to the bleeding Lamb.

17　　　　　　C. M.

HOW sweet the name of Jesus sounds
　　　　In a believer's ear !
It soothes his sorrows, heals his wounds,
　　And drives away his fear.

2 It makes the wounded spirit whole,
　　And calms the troubled breast;
'Tis manna to the hungry soul,
　　And to the weary rest.

3 Dear Name, the rock on which I build,
　　My shield and hiding place ;
My never failing treasury, filled
　　With boundless stores of grace.

4 Jesus, my Shepherd, Husband, Friend,
　　My Prophet, Priest and King;
My Lord, my Life, my Way, my End,
　　Accept th praise I bring.

5 Weak is the effort of my heart.
   And cold my warmest thought ;
But when I see thee as thou art,
   I'll praise thee as I ought.

6 Till then I would thy love proclaim
   With every fleeting breath ;
And may the music of thy name
   Refresh my soul in death.

18   C. M.

JESUS I love thy charming name,
   'Tis music to mine ear ;
Fain would I sound it out so loud,
   That earth and heaven should hear.

2 Yes, thou art precious to my soul,
   My joy, my hope, my trust ;
Jewels, to thee, are gaudy toys,
   And gold is sordid dust.

3 All my capacious powers can wish,
   In thee most richly meet ;
Nor to mine eye is light so dear,
   Nor friendship half so sweet.

4 Thy grace still dwells upon my heart,
   And sheds its fragrance there ;
The noblest balm of all its wounds,
   The cordial of its care.   B

5 I'll speak the honors of thy name,
    With my last, laboring breath;
  Then speechless clasp thee in mine arms,
    The antidote of death.

19   S. M.

NOT all the blood of beasts,
      On Jewish altars slain,
  Could give the guilty conscience peace,
    Or wash away the stain.

2 But Christ, the heavenly Lamb,
    Takes all our sins away;
  A sacrifice of nobler name,
    And richer blood than they.

3 My faith would lay her hand
    On that dear head of thine,
  While like a penitent, I stand,
    And there confess my sin.

4 My soul looks back to see
    The burdens thou didst bear,
  When hanging on the cursed tree,
    And hopes her guilt was there.

5 Believing, we rejoice
    To see the curse remove:
  We bless the Lamb with cheerful voice,
    And sing his bleeding love.

20   C. M.

OH, for a thousand tongues to sing
    My dear Redeemer's praise;
The glories of my God and King,
    The triumphs of his grace.

2 Jesus, the name that calms our fears,
    That bids our sorrows cease;
'Tis music in the sinner's ears:
    'Tis life, and health, and peace.

3 He breaks the power of reigning sin,
    He sets the prisoners free;
His blood can make the foulest clean,
    His blood availed for me.

4 Let us obey, we then shall know
    Shall feel our sins forgiven:
Anticipate our heaven below,
    And own that love is heaven.

21   8 s & 7 s.

ONE there is, above all others,
    Well deserves the name of friend;
His is love beyond a brother's,
    Costly, free, and knows no end:
They who once his kindness prove,
Find it everlasting love.

2 Which of all our friends to save us,
    Could or would have shed his blood?

But this Saviour died to have us
　　Reconciled in him to God:
This was boundless love indeed;
Jesus is a friend in need.

3　When he lived on earth abased,
　　Friend of sinners was his name;
Now above all glory raised,
　　He rejoices in the same:
Still he calls them brethren, friends,
And to all their wants attends.　　　•

4　Oh! for grace our hearts to soften;
　　Teach us, Lord, at length to love;
We, alas! forget too often,
　　What a Friend we have above:
But, when home our souls are brought,
We will love thee as we ought.

22　　　　　　　　7 s.

ROCK of ages, cleft for me,
　　Let me hide myself in thee;
Let the water and the blood,
From thy wounded side which flow'd,
Be of sin the double cure;
Cleanse me from its guilt and power.

2　Not the labor of my hands
Can fulfil the law's demands;
Could my zeal no respite know,
Could my tears forever flow,

All for sin could not atone,
Thou must save, and thou alone.

3 Nothing in my hand I bring,
Simply to thy cross I cling;
Naked, come to thee for dress,
Helpless, look to thee for grace;
Vile, I to the fountain fly.
Wash me, Saviour, or I die.

4 While I draw this fleeting breath,
When my eyelids close n death,
When I soar to worlds unknown,
See thee on thy judgment, throne:
Rock of ages, cleft for me,
Let me hide myself in thee.

23   L. M.

JESUS, and shall it ever be,
     A mortal man ashamed of thee?
Ashamed of thee, whom angels praise,
Whose glories shine through endless days!

2 Ashamed of Jesus! sooner far
  Let evening blush to own a star;
He sheds the beams of light divine,
O'er this benighted soul of mine.

3 Ashamed of Jesus! just as soon
Let midnight be ashamed of noon;
'Tis midnight with my soul, till He,
Bright Morning Star, bid darkness flee.

4 Ashamed of Jesus! that dear friend
  On whom my hopes of heaven depend!
  No, when I blush, be this my shame,
  That I no more revere his name.

5 Ashamed of Jesus! Yes, I may,
  When I've no guilt to wash away,
  No tear to wipe, no good to crave,
  No fears to quell, no soul to save.

6 Till then—nor is my boasting vain—
  Till then, I boast a Saviour slain:
  And O may this my glory be,
  That Christ is not ashamed of me.

24　　　　　　C. M.

THERE is a fountain fill'd with blood,
    Drawn from Immanuel's veins;
And sinner's, plunged beneath that flood,
    Lose all their guilty stains.

2 The dying thief rejoiced to see
    That fountain in his day;
And there may I, though vile as he,
    Wash all my sins away.

3 Dear dying Lamb, thy precious blood
    Shall never lose its power,
Till all the ransom'd church of God
    Be saved to sin no more.

4 E'er since by faith I saw the stream
    Thy flowing wounds supply;

Redeeming love has been my theme,
And shall be till I die.

5 Then in a nobler, sweeter song,
.I'll sing thy power to save;
When this poor lisping, stammering tongue
Lies silent in the grave.

25   L. M.

'TWAS on that dark, that doleful night,
    When powers of earth and hell arose
Against the Son of God's delight,
And friends betrayed Him to his foes.

2 Before the mournful scene began,
    He took the bread, and blessed and brake;
What love through all his actions ran!
    What wondrous words of grace He spake!

3 " This is my body broke for sin ;
    Receive and eat the living food;"
Then took the cup and blessed the wine,
    "'Tis the new covenant in my blood."

4 " Do this, (He cried,) 'till time shall end,
    In memory of your dying Friend ;
Meet at my table, and record
    The love of your departed Lord."

5 Jesus, thy feast we celebrate,
    We show thy death, we sing thy name,
'Till thou return, and we shall eat
    The marriage supper of the Lamb.

26   L. M.

WHEN I survey the wondrous cross,
    On which the Prince of glory died,
My richest gain I count but loss,
    And pour contempt on all my pride.

Forbid it, Lord, that I should boast,
    Save in the death of Christ, my God:
All the vain things that charm me most,
    I sacrifice them to his blood.

3 See, from his head, his hands, his feet,
    Sorrow and love flow mingled down;
Did e'er such love and sorrow meet,
    Or thorns compose so rich a crown?

4 Were the whole realm of nature mine,
    That were a present far too small;
Love so amazing, so Divine,
    Demands my soul, my life, my all.

THE BELIEVER.

27   C. M.

AM I a soldier of the cross,
    A follower of the Lamb,
And shall I fear to own his cause,
    Or blush to speak his name?

2 Must I be carried to the skies,
    On flowery beds of ease;

While others fought to win the prize,
And sailed through bloody seas?

3 Are there no foes for me to face?
Must I not stem the flood?
Is this dark world a friend to grace,
To help me on to God?

4 Sure I must fight, if I would reign;
Increase my courage, Lord;
I'll bear the toil, endure the pain,
Supported by thy word.

5 Thy saints in all this glorious war,
Shall conquer though they die;
They see the triumph from afar,
With faith's discerning eye.

6 When that illustrious day shall rise,
And all thine armies shine,
In robes of victory through the skies,
The glory shall be thine.

23   S. M.

BEHOLD what wondrous grace
    The Father hath bestow'd
On sinners of a mortal race,
    To call them sons of God!

2 Nor doth it yet appear
    How great we must be made:
But when we see our Saviour here,
    We shall be like our Head.

3 A hope so much divine
   May trials well endure,
May purge our souls from sense and sin,
   As Christ the Lord is pure.

4 If in my Father's love
   I share a filial part,
Send down thy Spirit like a dove
   To rest upon my heart.

5 We would no longer lie
   Like slaves beneath the throne;
My faith shall Abba, Father, cry,
   And thou the kindred own.

29   7 s.

CHILDREN of the heavenly King,
   As ye journey, sweetly sing:
Sing your Saviour's worthy praise,
Glorious in his works and ways.

2 Ye are travelling home to God,
   In the way the fathers trod ;
They are happy now, and ye
   Soon their happiness shall see.

3 O ye mourning souls be glad;
   Christ our advocate is made;
Us to save, our flesh assumes,
Brother to our souls becomes.

4 Shout, ye little flock, and blest,
   Soon you'll enter into rest ;

There your seat is now prepared,
There your kingdom and reward.

5 Fear not, brethren, joyful stand
On the borders of your land;
Jesus Christ, our Father's son,
Bids us undismayed go on.

6 Lord submissive make us go,
Gladly leaving all below;
Only thou our leader be,
And we still will follow thee.

30   8 s, 7 s & 4 s.

GUIDE me, O thou great Jehovah,
    Pilgrim through this barren land;
I am weak, but thou art mighty,
Hold me by thy powerful hand:
        Bread of heaven,
Feed me till I want no more.

2 Open now the crystal fountain,
    Whence the healing streams do flow;
Let the fiery cloudy pillar
Lead me all my journey through:
        Strong Deliverer,
Be thou still my strength and shield.

3 When I tread the verge of Jordan,
    Bid my anxious fears subside:
Death of death, and hell's destruction,
Land me safe on Canaan's side:
        Songs of praises
I will ever give to thee.

31   'C. M.

I'M not ashamed to own my Lord,
    Or to defend his cause,
Maintain the honor of his word,
    The glory of his cross.

2 Jesus, my God, I know his name,
    His name is all my trust;
Nor will he put my soul to shame,
    Nor let my hope be lost.

3 Firm as his throne his promise stands,
    And he can well secure
What I've committed to his hands,
    Till the decisive hour.

4 Then will he own my worthless name,
    Before his Father's face,
And in the New Jerusalem,
    Appoint my soul a place.

32   C. M.

IN all my Lord's appointed ways
    My journey I'll pursue;
Hinder me not, ye much loved saints,
    For I must go with you.

2 Through floods and flames, if Jesus lead,
    I'll follow where he goes;
Hinder me not, shall be my cry,
    Though earth and hell oppose.

3 Through duty, and through trials, too,
　I'll go at his command :
　Hinder me not, for I am bound
　To my Immanuel's land.

4 And when my Saviour calls me home,
　My joyful cry shall be,
　Hinder me not, come, welcome death ;
　I'll gladly go with thee.

33　　　　　　L. M.

JESUS, my all, to heaven is gone,
　　He, whom I fixed my hopes upon ;
His track I see, and I'll pursue
The narrow way,. till him I view.

2 The way the holy prophets went,
　The road that leads from banishment,
　The King's highway of holiness
　I'll go, for all his paths are peace.

3 This is the way I long have sought,
　And mourned because I found it not ;
　My grief and burden long have been,
　Because I could not cease from sin.

4 The more I strove against its power,
　I sinned and stumbled but the more,
　Till late I heard my Saviour say,
　"Come hither, soul, I am the way."

5 Lo ! glad I come, and thou, blest Lamb,
　Shalt take me to thee as I am :

Nothing but sin I thee can give,
Nothing but love shall I receive.

6 Then will I sing to sinners round,
What a dear Saviour I have found,
I'll point to thy redeeming blood,
And say—"Behold the way to God!"

34   S. M.

MY soul be on thy guard,
    Ten thousand foes arise;
And hosts of sin are pressing hard
    To draw thee from the skies.

2 O watch, and fight, and pray,
    The battle ne'er give o'er;
Renew it boldly every day,
    And help divine implore.

3 Ne'er think the victory won,
    Nor once at ease sit down;
Thy arduous work will not be done,
    Till thou hast got thy crown.

35   C. M.

O! FOR a closer walk with God,
    A calm and Heavenly frame;
A light to shine upon the road
    That leads me to the Lamb.

2 Where is the blessedness I knew
  When first I saw the Lord?
Where is the soul-refreshing view
  Of Jesus and his word?

3 What peaceful hours I once enjoyed,
  How sweet their memory still!
But they have left an aching void,
  The world can never fill.

4 Return, O holy Dove, return,
  Sweet messenger of rest;
I hate the sins that made thee mourn,
  And drove thee from my breast.

5 The dearest idol I have known,
  Whate'er that idol be,
Help me to tear it from thy throne,
  And worship only thee.

6 So shall my walk be close with God,
  Calm and serene my frame;
So purer light shall mark the road
  That leads me to the Lamb.

36   C. M.

OH that the Lord would guide my ways,
  To keep his statutes still!
Oh that my God would grant me grace,
  To know and do his will!

2 Oh send thy Spirit down, to write
  Thy law upon my heart

Nor let my tongue indulge deceit,
  Nor act the liar's part.

3 Order my footsteps by thy word,
    And make my heart sincere:
  Let sin have no dominion, Lord,
    But keep my conscience clear.

4 Make me to walk in thy commands;
    'Tis a delightful road;
  Nor let my head, or heart, or hands,
    Offend against my God.

37   O. M.

SALVATION! Oh, the joyful sound;
    'Tis pleasure to our ears;
  A sovereign balm for every wound,
    A cordial for our fears.

2 Buried in sorrow and in sin,
    At hell's dark door we lay;
  But we arise by grace Divine,
    To see a heavenly day.

3 Salvation! let the echo fly
    The spacious earth around;
  While all the armies of the sky
    Conspire to raise the sound.

4 Now let the Father and the Son
    And Spirit be adored,
  Where there are works to make him known,
    Or saints to love the Lord.

38 C. M.

PLUNGED in a gulf of dark despair,
  We wretched sinners lay,
Without one. cheerful beam of hope,
  Or spark of glimmering day.

2 With pitying eyes, the Prince of grace
  Beheld our helpless grief:
He saw, and, O amazing love!
  He ran to our relief.

4 Down from the shining seats above,
  With joyful haste He. fled;
Entered the grave in mortal flesh,
  And dwelt among the dead.

4 He spoiled the powers of darkness thus,
  And brake our iron chains;
Jesus has freed our captive souls
  From everlasting pains.

5 O! for this love, let rocks and hills
  Their lasting silence break;
And all harmonious human tongues
  The Saviour's praises speak.·

THE SINNER.

39 L. C. M.

AWAKED by Sinai's awful sound,
  My soul in bonds of guilt I found,
And knew not where to go;
  C

Eternal truth did loud proclaim,
"The sinner must be born again,
 Or sink to endless woe."

2 When to the law I trembling fled,
It poured its curses on my head,
 I no relief could find;
This fearful truth increased my pain,
"The sinner must be born again,"
 And whelmed my tortured mind.

3 Again did Sinai's thunder roll,
And guilt lay heavy on my soul,
 A vast oppressive load;
Alas, I read and saw it plain,
"The sinner must be born again,
 Or drink the wrath of God."

4 The saints I heard with rapture tell,
How Jesus conquered death and hell,
 And broke the fowler's snare;
Yet when I found this truth remain,
"The sinner must be born again,"
 I sunk in deep despair.

5 But while I thus in anguish lay,
The gracious Saviour passed this way,
 And felt his pity move;
The sinner, by his justice slain,
Now by his grace is born again,
 And sings redeeming love.

40 11 s.

DELAY not, delay not, O sinner, draw near;
The waters of life are now flowing for thee
No price is demanded, the Saviour is here,
Redemption is purchased, salvation is free.

2 Delay not, delay not, why longer abuse
The love and compassion of Jesus thy God?
A fountain is opened, how canst thou refuse
To wash and be cleansed in his pardoning
blood?

3 Delay not, delay not, O sinner, to come,
For mercy still lingers, and calls thee to-day:
Her voice is not heard in the vale of the tomb;
Her message unheeded will soon pass away.

4 Delay not, delay not, the Spirit of Grace,
Long grieved and resisted, may take its sad
flight;
And leave thee in darkness to finish thy race,
To sink in the gloom of eternity's night.

6 Delay not, delay not, the hour is at hand;
The earth shall dissolve, and the heavens
shall fade;
The dead, small and great, in the judgment
shall stand;
What power then, O sinner, shall lend thee
its aid?

41   L. M.

HASTEN, O sinner, to be wise,
    And stay not for to-morrow's sun;
The longer Wisdom you despise,
    The harder is she to be won.

2 O! hasten mercy to implore,
    And stay not for to-morrow's sun;
For fear thy season should be o'er,
    Before this evening's course be run.

3 Hasten, O sinner, to return,
    And stay not for to-morrow's sun,
For fear thy lamp should fail to burn,
    Before the needful work is done.

Hasten, O sinner, to be blest,
    And stay not for to-morrow's sun;
For fear the curse should thee arrest,
    Before the morrow is begun.

42   S. M.

O WHERE shall rest be found,
    Rest for the weary soul?
'Twere vain the ocean depths to sound,
    Or pierce to either pole:
The world can never give
    The bliss for which we sigh;
'Tis not the whole of life to live,
    Nor all of death to die.

2 Beyond this vale of tears
    There is a life above,
Unmeasured by the flight of years;
    And all that life is love.
There is a death whose pang
  • Outlasts the fleeting breath ;
O what eternal horrors hang
    Around "the second death !"

3 Lord God of truth and grace,
    Teach us that death to shun,
Lest we be banished from thy face,
    And evermore undone.
Here would we end our quest :
    Alone are found in thee,
The life of perfect love, the rest
    Of immortality.

43   L. M.

SAY, sinner, hath a voice within,
    Oft whispered to thy secret soul ;
Urged thee to leave the ways of sin,
    And yield thy heart to God's control ?

2 Hath something met thee in the path
    Of worldliness and vanity,
And pointed to the coming wrath,
    And warned thee from that wrath to flee ?

3 Sinner, it was a heavenly voice,
    It was the Spirit's gracious call ;

It bade thee make the better choice,
And haste to seek in Christ thine all,

4 Spurn not the call to life and light;
Regard in time the warning kind;
That call thou may'st not always sight,
And yet the gate of mercy find.   •

5 God's Spirit will not always strive
With hardened, self-destroying man;
Ye who persist his love to grieve,
May never hear his voice again.

6 Sinner, perhaps this very day,
Thy last accepted time may be;
O should'st thou grieve him now away,
Then hope may never beam on thee.

44   7 s.

SINNER, art thou still secure?
Wilt thou still refuse to pray?
Can thy heart or hand endure,
In the Lord's avenging day?

2 See, his mighty arm is bared,
Awful terrors clothe his brow;
For his judgment stand prepared;
Thou must either break or bow.

3 At his presence nature shakes,
Earth, affrighted, hastes to flee;

Solid mountains melt like wax,
    What will then become of thee!

4 Who his coming may abide,
    You that glory in your shame?
Will you find a place to hide, •
    When the world is wrapped in flame!

5 Lord, prepare us by thy grace ;
    Soon we must resign our breath,
And our souls be called to pass
    Through the iron gate of death.

45   S. M.

TO-MORROW, Lord, is thine,
        Lodged in thy Sovereign hand,
And if its sun arise and shine,
    It shines by thy command.

2 The present moment flies,
    And bears our life away ;
Oh make thy servants truly wise,
    That they may live to-day.

3 Since on this fleeting hour
    Eternity is hung,
Waken by thine almighty power
    The aged and the young.

4 One thing demands our care ;
    Oh be it still pursued ;
Lest slighted once, the season fair
    Should never be renew'd.

5 To Jesus may we fly,
   Swift as the morning light ;
.Lest life's young golden beam should die
   In sudden endless night.

46   **L. M.**

WHILE life prolongs its precious light,
   Mercy is found, and peace is given;
But soon, ah ! soon, approaching night
   Shall blot out every hope of heaven.

2 While God invites, how blest the day !
   How sweet the gospel's charming sound ;
Come sinners, haste, oh! haste away,
   While yet a pardoning God He's found.

3 Soon, borne on time's most rapid wing,
   Shall death command you to the grave ;
Before his bar your spirits bring,
   And none be found to hear or save.

4 In that lone land of deep despair,
   No Sabbath's heavenly light shall rise ;
No God regard your bitter prayer,
   Nor Saviour call you to the skies.

5 While God invites—how blest the day !
   How sweet the gospel's charming sound ;
Come, sinners haste, oh! haste away,
   While yet a pard'ning God is found.

THE PENITE·NT.

47　　　　　C. M.

COME; humble sinner, in whose breast
　　A thousand thoughts revolve;
Come, with your guilt and fear oppressed,
And make this last resolve:

2 I'll go to Jesus, though my sin
　　Hath like a mountain rose:
I know his courts, I'll enter in,
Whatever may oppose.

3 Perhaps he will admit my plea,
　　Perhaps will hear my prayer;
But if I perish I will pray,
And perish only there.

4 I can but perish if I go,
　　I am resolved to try;
For if I stay away, I know
I must for ever die.

48　　　　　C. M. D.

I HEARD the voice of Jesus say,
　　Come unto me and rest;
Lay down, thou weary one, lay down
　　Thy head upon my breast.
I came to Jesus as I was,
　　Weary, and worn, and sad,

I found in Him a resting place,
    And He has made me glad.

2 I heard the voice of Jesus say,
      Behold, I freely give
The living water, thirsty one,
    Stoop down, and drink, and live.
I came to Jesus, and I drank
    Of that life-giving stream;
My thirst was quenched, my soul revived,
    And now I live in Him.

3 I heard the voice of Jesus say,
      I am this dark world's light,
Look unto me, thy morn shall rise,
    And all thy days be bright.
I looked to Jesus, and I found
    In Him my Star, my Sun;
And in that light of life I'll walk,
    Till travelling days are done.

49   S. M.

JESUS, I come to thee,
    A sinner doomed to die;
My only refuge is thy cross—
    Here at thy feet I lie.

2 Can mercy reach my case,
      And all my sins remove?
  Break, O my God! this heart of stone,
    And melt it by thy love,

3 Too long my soul has gone;
  *Far from my God, astray ;
• I've sported on the brink of hell,
    In sin's delusive way.

4 But, Lord ! my heart is fixed—
    I hope in thee alone ;
  Break off the chains of sin and death,
    And bind me to thy throne.

5 Thy blood can cleanse my heart,
    Thy hand can wipe my tears ;
  Oh ! send thy blessed Spirit down
    To banish all my fears.

6 Then shall my soul arise,
    From sin and Satan free ;
  Redeemed from hell and every foe,
    I'll trust alone in thee.

50   8, 8, 8, 6.

• JUST as I am—without one plea,
    But that thy blool was shed for me ;
  And that thou bidst me come to thee—.
    O Lamb of God, I come ?

2 Just as I am—and waiting not
  To rid my soul of one dark blot,
  To thee, whose blood can cleanse each spot,
    O Lamb of God, I come !

3 Just as I am—poor, wretched, blind ;
  Sight, riches, healing of the mind,

Yea, all I need in thee to find—
    O Lamb of God, I come!

4 Just as I am—thou wilt receive,
  Wilt welcome, pardon, cleanse, relieve,
  Because thy promise I believe—
    O Lamb of God, I come!

5 Just as I am—thy love unknown
  Has broken every barrier down;
  Now to be thine, yea, thine alone—
    O Lamb of God, I come!

51   C. M.

LET carnal minds the world pursue,
    It has no charms for me;
Once I admir'd its trifles too,
    But grace has set me free.

2 Its fading charms no longer please,
    No more content afford;
Far from my heart be joys like these,
    Now I have seen the Lord.

3 As by the light of op'ning day,
    The stars are all conceal'd;
So earthly pleasures fade away,
    When Jesus is reveal'd.

4 Creatures no more divide my choice—
    I bid them all depart;
His name, and love, and gracious voice,
    Have fix'd my roving heart.

Now, Lord, I would bo thine alone,
  And wholly live to thee ;
But may I hope that thou wilt own
  A worthless worm like me!

Yes, though of sinners I'm the worst,
  I cannot doubt thy will ;
For, if thou had'st not lov'd me first,
  I had refus'd thee still.

C. M.

PROSTRATE, dear Jesus, at thy feet,
  A guilty rebel lies ;
And upwards to thy mercy seat,
  Presumes to lift his eyes.

If tears of sorrow would suffice
  To pay the debt I owe,
Tears should from both my weeping eyes,
  In ceaseless torrents flow.

But no such sacrifice I plead
  To expiate my guilt ;
No tears but those which thou hast shed ;
  No blood, but thou hast spilt.

Think of thy sorrows, dearest Lord,
  And all my sins forgive :
Justice will well approve the word
  That bids the sinner live.

53   L. M.

O HAPPY day, that stays my cho'ce
    On thee, my Saviour and my God;
Well may this glowing heart rejoice,
    And tell thy goodness all abroad.

2 O happy bond, that seals my vows,
    To Him who merits all my love,
Let cheerful anthems fill his house,
    While to his sacred throne I move.

3 'Tis done, the great transaction's done;
    Deign, gracious Lord, to make me thine:
Help me, through grace, to follow on,
    Glad to confess thy voice divine.

4 Here rest, my oft-divided heart,
    Fix'd on thy God, thy Saviour, rest;
Who with the world would grieve to part,
    When call'd on angel's food to feast?

High heaven, that heard the solemn vow,
    That vow renew'd shall daily hear,
Till in life's latest hour I bow,
    And bless in death a bond so dear.

THE SABBATH.

54   L. M.

ANOTHER six days' work is done,
    Another Sabbath is begun;

Return, my soul, enjoy thy rest,
Improve the day that God has bless'd.

2 Oh that our thoughts and thanks may rise
As grateful incense to the skies;
And draw from heaven the sweet repose
Which none but he that feels it knows!

3 This heavenly calm within the breast
Is the dear pledge of glorious rest,
Which for the church of God remains,
The end of cares, the end of pains.

4 In holy duties let the day,
In holy pleasures pass away;
How sweet a Sabbath thus to spend,
In hope of one that ne'er shall end!

55   C. M.

FREQUENT the day of God returns,
    To shed its quickening beams;
And yet how slow devotion burns,
    How languid are its flames!

2 Accept our faint attempts to love;
    Our frailties, Lord forgive:
We would be like thy saints above,
    And praise thee while we live.

3 Increase, O Lord, our faith and hope,
    And fit us to ascend,
Where the assembly ne'er breaks up,
    The Sabbath ne'er shall end.

4 Where we shall breathe in heavenly air,
    With heavenly lustre shine ;
Before the throne of God appear,
    And feast on love divine.

56   C. L. M.

HOW calm and beautiful the morn
    That gilds the sacred tomb,
Where once the Crucified was borne,
    And veiled in midnight gloom !
O weep no more the Saviour slain ;
The Lord is risen—He lives again.

2 Ye mourning saints, dry every tear
    For your departed Lord ;
"Behold the place—He is not here,"
    The tomb is all unbarred ;
The gates of death were closed in vain ;
The Lord is risen—He lives again.

3 Now cheerful to the house of prayer,
    Your early footsteps bend,
The Saviour will himself be there,
    Your Advocate and Friend :
Once by the law your hopes were slain,
But now in Christ ye live again.

4 How tranquil now the rising day,
    'Tis Jesus still appears,
A risen Lord to chase away
    Your unbelieving fears :
O weep no more your comforts slain ;
The Lord is risen—He lives again.

5 And when the shades of evening fall,
  When life's last hour draws nigh,
If Jesus shines upon the soul,
  How blissful then to die!
Since He has risen who once was slain,
Ye die in Christ to live again.

MORNING AND EVENING.

57   C. M.

DREAD Sovereign, let my evening song
    Like holy incense rise:
Assist the offerings of my tongue,
    To reach the lofty skies.

2 Through all the dangers of the day,
    Thy hand was still my guard;
And still to drive my wants away
    Thy mercy stood prepared.

3 Perpetual blessings from above,
    Encompassed me around;
But O how few returns of love
    Has my Creator found!

4 What have I done for Him who died
    To save my wretched soul?
How are my follies multiplied,
    Fast as my minutes roll!

5 Lord, with this guilty heart of mine,
    To thy dear cross I flee,   D

And to thy grace my soul resign,
To be renewed by thee.

58   C. M.

LORD, thou wilt hear me when I pray;
    I am forever thine :
I fear before thee all the day,
    Nor would I dare to sin.

2 And while I rest my weary head
    From cares and business free,
'Tis sweet conversing on my bed
    With my own heart and thee.

3 I pay this evening sacrifice;
    And when my work is done,
Great God, my faith and hope relies
    Upon thy grace alone.

4 Thus, with my thoughts composed to peace,
    I'll give mine eyes to sleep;
Thy hand in safety keeps my days,
    And will my slumbers keep.

59   .   C. M.

LORD in the morning thou shalt hear
    My voice ascending high;
To Thee will I direct my prayer,
    To Thee lift up mine eye:

2 Up to the hills where Christ is gone,
    To plead for all his saints,

Presenting at his Father's throne
Our songs and our complaints.

3 Thou art a God, before whose sight
  The wicked shall not stand;
Sinners shall ne'er be thy delight,
  Nor dwell at thy right hand.

4 O may thy Spirit guide my feet,
  In ways of righteousness!
Make ev'ry path of duty straight,
  And plain before my face.

60   7 s.

NOW the shades of night are gone;
    Now the morning light is come;
Lord, may we be thine to-day,
Drive the shades of sin away.

2 Fill our souls with heavenly light,
Banish doubt and gloomy night;
In thy service, Lord, to-day,
Help us labor, help us pray.

3 Keep our haughty passions bound;
Save us from our foes around;
Going out, and coming in,
Keep us safe from every sin.

4 When our work of life is past,
O receive us then at last!
Night of sin will be no more,
When we reach the heavenly shore.

61   C. M.

O LORD, another day is flown,
    And we, a little band,
Are met once more before thy throne,
    To bless thy fostering hand.

2 And wilt thou bend a listening ear,
    To praises low as ours?
Thou wilt, for thou dost deign to hear
    The songs that meekness pours.

3 And Jesus, thou thy smiles wilt deign,
    As we before thee pray;
For thou didst bless the infant train,
    And we are less than they.

4 O let thy grace peform its part;
    Let sin's dominion cease;
And shed abroad in every heart,
    Thine everlasting peace.

62   8 s & 7 s.

SAVIOUR, breathe an evening blessing,
    Ere repose our spirits seal;
Sin and want we come confessing,
    Thou canst save and thou canst heal.
Though destruction walk around us,
    Though the arrow near us fly,
Angel-guards from thee surround us,
    We are safe if thou art nigh.

2 Though the night be dark and dreary,
  Darkness cannot hide from thee ;
Thou art He who, never weary,
  Watchest where thy people be.
Should swift death this night o'ertake us,
  And our couch become our tomb,
May the morn, in heaven awake us,
  Clad in light and deathless bloom.

DEATH AND THE JUDGMENT.

63   C. M.

HEAR what the voice from heaven proclaims,
  For all the pious dead ;
Sweet is the savor of their names,
  And soft their sleeping bed.

2 They die in Jesus, and are bless'd ;
  How kind their slumbers are !
From sufferings and from sin released.
  And freed from every snare.

3 Far from this world of toil and strife,
  They're present with the Lord ;
The labors of their mortal life
  End in a large reward.

64   8 s, 7 s & 4 s.

LO ! he comes, with clouds descending,
  Once for favored sinners slain ;

Thousand thousand saints attending,
Swell the triumph of his train.
Hallelujah!
Jesus comes, and comes to reign.

2 Every eye shall now behold him,
Robed in dreadful majesty:
Those who set at nought and sold him,
Pierc'd and nail'd him to the tree,
Deeply wailing,
Shall the true Messiah see.

3 Now redemption, long expected,
See in solemn pomp appear:
All his saints, by man rejected,
Now shall meet him in the air.
Hallelujah!
See the day of God appear.

4 Mighty King, let all adore Thee,
High on thine eternal throne;
Saviour, take the power and glory,
Claim the kingdom for thine own.
Oh, come quickly!
Hallelujah! come, Lord, come!

65   L. C. M.

LO! on a narrow neck of land,
'Twixt two unbounded seas I stand,
Yet how insensible!
A point of time, a moment's space,

Removes me to yon heavenly place,
Or shuts me up in hell.

2 O God my inmost soul convert,
And deeply on my thoughtless heart,
Eternal things impress;
Give me to feel their solemn weight,
And save me ere it be too late;
Wake me to righteousness.

3 Before me place in bright array,
The pomp of that tremendous day,
When thou with clouds shall come
To judge the nations at thy bar:
And tell me, Lord, shall I be there,
To meet a joyful doom?

4 Be this my one great business here,
With holy trembling, holy fear,
To make my calling sure;
Thine utmost counsel to fulfil,
And suff'r all thy righteous will,
And to the end endure.

5 Then, Saviour, then my soul receive,
Transported from this vale, to live
And reign with thee above;
Where faith is sweetly lost in sight,
And hope, in full, supreme delight,
And everlasting love.

66   C. M.

WHEN rising from the bed of death,
O'erwhelmed with guilt and fear,

I see my Maker face to face,
  O how shall I appear?

2 If yet while pardon may be found,
  And mercy may be sought,
My heart with inward horror shrinks,
  And trembles at the thought;

3 When thou, O Lord, shalt stand disclosed,
  In majesty severe,
And sit in judgment on my soul,
  O how shall I appear?

4 Yet never shall my soul despair
  Her pardon to procure,
Who knows thine only Son has died,
  To make her pardon sure.

67   C. M.

WHY do we mourn departed friends,
  Or shake at death's alarms?
'Tis but the voice that Jesus sends,
  To call them to his arms.

2 Are we not tending upward too,
  As fast as time can move?
Nor should we wish our hours more slow,
  To keep us from our love.

3 Why should we tremble to convey
  Their bodies to the tomb?
There the dear flesh of Jesus lay,
  And left a long perfume.

4 The graves of all the saints He blest,
   And softened every bed;
   Where should the dying members rest,
   But with their dying Head?

5 Thence He arose, ascending high,
   And showed our feet the way;
   Up to the Lord our flesh shall fly,
   At the great rising day.

68   • L. M.

WHY should we start and fear to die?
     What timorous worms we mortals are!
Death is the gate to endless joy.
   And yet we dread to enter there.

2 The pains, the groans and dying strife,
   Fright our approaching souls away;
Still we shrink back again to life,
   Fond of our prison and our clay.

3 O if my Lord would come and meet,
   My soul would stretch her wings in haste,
Fly fearless through death's iron gate,
   Nor feel the terrors as she passed.

4 Jesus can make a dying bed
   Feel soft as downy pillows are,
While on his breast I lean my head,
   And breathe my life out sweetly there.

TRIALS.

69   **S. M.**

GIVE to the winds thy fears;
   Hope on, be not dismayed;
God hears thy sighs and counts thy tears;
   God shall lift up thy head.

2 Through waves, and clouds and storms
   He gently clears thy way;
Wait thou his time: the darkest night
   Shall end in brightest day.

3 Far, far above thy thought
   His counsels shall appear,
When fully he the work hath wrought
   That caused thy needless fear.

4 What though thou rulest not!
   Yet heaven, and earth, and hell
Proclaim—God sitteth on the throne,
   And ruleth all things well.

70   **8 s & 7 s.**

GENTLY, Lord, O! gently lead us,
   Through this lonely vale of tears;
Through the changes thou'st decreed us,
   Till our last great change appears.
When temptation's darts assail us,
   When in devious paths we stray,

Let thy goodness never fail us,
  Lead us in thy perfect way.

2 In the hour of pain and anguish,
  In the hour when death draws near,
Suffer not our hearts to languish,
  Suffer not our souls to fear.
And when mortal life is ended,
  Bid us in thine arms to rest,
Till by angel bands attended,
  We awake among the blest.

71   L. M.

GOD is the refuge of His saints,
  When storms of sharp distress invade;
Ere we can offer our complaints,
  Behold Him present with His aid.

2 Let mountains from their seats be hurled,
  Down to the deep and buried there;
Convulsions shake the solid world,
  Our faith shall never yield to fear.

3 Loud may the troubled ocean roar,
  In sacred peace our souls abide;
While ev'ry nation, ev'ry shore,
  Trembles and dreads the swelling tide.

4 There is a stream, whose gentle flow
  Supplies the city of our God;
Life, love, and joy, still gliding through,
  And wat'ring our divine abode.

5 That sacred stream, thine, holy word,
    Supports our faith, our fear controls;
Sweet peace thy promises afford,
    And give new strength to fainting souls.

6 Zion enjoys her monarch's love,
    Secure against a threat'ning hour;
Nor can her firm foundations move,
    Built on his truth, and armed with power.

72 .   L. M.

HOW oft have sin and Satan strove
    To rend my soul from thee, my God!
But everlasting is thy love,
    And Jesus seals it with his blood.

2 The oath and promise of the Lord
    Join to confirm the wondrous grace;
Eternal power performs the word,
    And fills all heaven with endless praise.

3 Amidst temptations sharp and long
    My soul to this dear refuge flies:
Hope is my anchor, firm and strong,
    While tempests blow, and billows rise.

4 The gospel bears my spirit up;
    A faithful and unchanging God
Lays the foundation for my hope
    In oaths, and promises, and blood.

73 • 7 s.

JESUS, lover of my soul,
　Let me to thy bosom fly,
While the ·raging billows roll,
　While the tempest still is high.
Hide me, O my Saviour, hide,
　Till the storm of life is past;
Safe into the haven guide;
　O receive my soul at last.

2 Other refuge have I none,
　Hangs my helpless soul on thee;
Leave, ah! leave me not alone,
　Still support and comfort me;
All my trust on thee is staid,
　All my help from thee I bring;
Cover my defenceless head,
　With the shadow of thy wing.

3 Thou, O Christ, art all I want;
　All in all in thee I find,
Raise the fallen, cheer the faint,
　Heal the sick, and lead the blind;
Just and holy is thy name,
　I am all unrighteousness;
Vile and full of sin I am,
　Thou art full of truth and grace.

4 Plenteous grace with thee is found,
　Grace to pardon all my sin;
Let the healing streams abound,
　Make and keep me pure within.

Thou of life the fountain art,
Freely let me take of thee:
Spring thou up within my heart,
Rise to all eternity.

74   C. M.

O THOU from whom all goodness flows,
I lift my soul to thee;
In all my sorrows, conflicts, woes,
O Lord, remember me!

2 When on my aching, burdened heart
My sins lie heavily,
Thy pardon grant, new peace impart;
Then, Lord, remember me;

3 When trials sore obstruct my way,
And ills I cannot flee,
Oh, let my strength be as my day—
Dear Lord, remember me!

4 When in the so'emn hour of death
I wait thy just decree;
Be this the prayer of my last breath:
Now, Lord, remember me!

75   L. M.

WHEN sins and fears prevailing rise,
And fainting hope almost expires,
Jesus, to thee I lift mine eyes,
To thee I breathe my soul's desires.

2 Art thou not mine, my living Lord?
 And can my hope, my comfort die,
Fixed on thy everlasting word.
 That word which built the earth and sky?

3 If my immortal Saviour lives,
 Then my immortal life is sure; . .
His word a firm foundation gives,
 Here let me build and rest secure.
 ⋮

4 Here let my faith unshaken dwell,.
 Immovable the promise stands;
Nor all the powers of earth, or hell,
 Can e'er dissolve the sacred bands.

5 Here, O, my soul, thy trust repose;
 Since Jesus is forever mine,
Not. death itself, that last of foes,
 Shall break a union so divine.

76 · 11 s.

HOW firm a foundation, ye saints of the
 Lord,
Is laid for your faith in his excellent word!
What more can He say than to you he hath
 said,
You who unto Jesus for refuge have fled?

2 In every condition—in sickness, in health,
In poverty's vale, or abounding in wealth,
At home and abroad, on the land, on the sea,
"As thy days may demand, shall thy strength
 ever be.

3 "Fear not, I am with thee! O! be not dis-
       mayed,
   I, I am thy God, and will still give thee aid;
   I'll strengthen thee, help thee, and cause thee
       to stand,
   Upheld by my righteous, omnipotent hand.

4 "When through the deep waters I call thee
       to go,
   The rivers of wo shall not thee overflow;
   For I will be with thee thy troubles to bless,
   And sanctify to thee, thy deepest distress.

5 "When through fiery trials thy pathway shall
       lie,
   My grace all-sufficient shall be thy supply;
   The flame shall not hurt thee; I only design
   Thy dross to consume, and thy gold to refine.

6 "E'en down to old age, all my people shall
       prove
   My sovereign, eternal, unchangeable love;
   And when hoary hairs shall their temples
       adorn,
   Like lambs they shall still in my bosom be
       borne.

7 "The soul that on Jesus hath leaned for re-
       pose,
   I will not, I will not, desert to his foes;
   That soul, though all hell should endeavor to
   shake,
   I'll never, no never, no never forsake!"

THE HOLY SPIRIT.

77 C. M.

COME, Holy Spirit heavenly Dove,
    With all thy quickening powers;
Kindle a flame of sacred love
    In these cold hearts of ours.

2 Look, how we grovel here below,
    Fond of these trifling toys:
Our souls can neither fly nor go
    To reach eternal joys.

3 Dear Lord! and shall we ever live
    At this poor dying rate?
Our love so faint, so cold to thee,
    And thine to us so great?

4 Come, Holy Spirit, heavenly Dove,
    With all thy quickening powers;
Come, shed abroad a Saviour's love,
    And that shall kindle ours.

78 S. M.

COME, holy Spirit! come,
    Let thy bright beams arise;
Dispel the sorrow from our minds,
    The darkness from our eyes.

2 Convince us of our sin,
    Then lead to Jesus' blood;

E

And to our wandering view reveal
The secret love of God.

3 'Tis thine to cleanse the heart,
To sanctify the soul:
To pour fresh life in every part,
And new create the whole.

4 Revive our drooping faith;
Our doubts and fears remove:
And kindle in our breast the flame
Of never dying love.

HEAVEN.

79   C. M.

JERUSALEM, my happy home,
Name ever dear to me!
When shall my labors have an end.
In joy, and peace and thee?

2 When shall these eyes thy heaven-built walls
And pearly g tes behold?
Thy bulwarks, with salvation strong,
And streets of shining gold?

3 O when, thou city of my God,
Shall I thy courts ascend,
Where congregations ne'er break up,
And Sabbaths have no end?

4 There happier bowers than Eden's bloom,
Nor sin nor sorrow know:

Blest seats, through rude and stormy scenes,
   I onward press to you.

5 - Why should I shrink at pain and woe,
   Or feel at death, dismay?
I've Canaan's goodly land in view,
   And realms of endless day.

6 Apostles, martyrs, prophets there
   Around my Saviour stand;
And soon my friends, in Christ, below,
   Will join the glorious band.

7 Jerusalem, my happy home,
   My soul still pants for thee:
Then shall my labors have an end,
   When I thy joys shall see.

80   C. M.

ON Jordan's stormy banks I stand,
   And cast a wishful eye
To Canaan's fair and happy land,
   Where my possessions lie.

2 O the transporting, rapturous scene,
   That rises to my sight;
Sweet fields arrayed in living green,
   And rivers of delight.

3 There generous fruits, that never fail,
   On trees immortal grow;
There rocks, and hills, and brooks, and vales
   With milk and honey flow.

4 On all those wide-extended plains
     Shines one eternal day;
   There God the Son for ever reigns,
     And scatters night away..

5 No chilling winds nor poisonous breath
     Can reach that healthful shore:
   Sickness and sorrow, pain and death,
     Are felt and feared no more.

81   C. M.

   THERE is a land of pure delight,
        Where saints immortal reign,
   Infinite day excludes the night,
        And pleasures banish pain.

2 There everlasting spring abides,
     And never withering flowers;
   Death, like a narrow sea, divides
     This heavenly land from ours.

3 Sweet fields beyond the swelling flood,
     Stand dressed in living green;
   So to the Jews old Canaan stood,
     While Jordan rolled between.

4 But timorous mortals start and shrink,
     To cross this narrow sea;
   And linger, shivering on the brink,
     And fear to launch away.

5 O could we make our doubts remove,
     Those gloomy doubts that rise,

And see the Canaan that we love
With unbeclouded eyes :

6 Could we but climb where Moses stood,
And view the landscape o'er ;
Not Jordan's stream, nor death's cold flood
Should frignt us from the shore.

82   C. M.

WHEN I can read my title clear
To mansions in the skies,
I bid farewell to every fear,
And wipe my weeping eyes.

2 Should earth against my soul engage,
And hellish darts be hurl'd
Then I can smile at Satan's rage,
And face a frowning world.

3 Let cares like a wild deluge come,
And storms of sorrow fall.
May I but safely reach my home.
My God, my heaven, my all !

4 There shall I bathe my weary soul
In seas of heavenly rest,
And not a wave of trouble roll
Across my peaceful breast.

DOXOLOGIES.

C. M.

LET God the Father, and the Son,
  And Spirit be adored,
Where there are works to make him known
Or saints to love the Lord.

C. M.

TO Father, Son, and Holy Ghost,
  The God whom we adore,
Be glory as it was, is now,
  And shall be evermore.

C. M. D.

THE God of mercy be adored,
  Who calls our souls from death,
Who saves by his redeeming Word,
  And new-creating Breath.

2 To praise the Father, and the Son,
  And Spirit, all divine,
The One in Three, and Three in One,
  Let saints and angels join.

L. M.

PRAISE God, from whom all blessings flow;
  Praise him, all creatures here below:
Praise him above, ye heavenly host;
Praise Father, Son, and Holy Ghost.

L. M.

TO God the Father, God tho Son,
 And God the Spirit, Three in One.
Be honor, praise, and glory given,
By all on earth, and all in heaven.

S. M.

YE angels round the throne,
 And saints that dwell below,
Worship the Father, love the Son.
And bless the Spirit too.

H. M.

TO God the Father's throne
 Perpetual honors raise;
Glory to God the Son,
 To God the Spirit praise:
With all our powers, eternal King,
Thy name we sing, while faith adores

7 s.

SING we to our God above,
 Praise eternal as his love:
Praise him, all ye heavenly host,
Father, Son, and Holy Ghost.

8 s, 7 s & 4 s.

GLORY be to God the Father,
 Glory to the eternal Son;
Sound aloud the Spirit's praises;
 Join the elders round the throne,
  Hallelujah,
Hail the glorious Three in One.

HYMNS.

INDEX· OF FIRST LINES.

THE NUMBERS REFER TO THE PAGES OF THE BOOK.

1. My days are gliding swiftly by, And I a pil-

g'm stran'r, W'ld not detain them as they fly! Those hours

of toil and danger, For oh! we st'nd'on Jordan's strand

Our friends are passing over, And just before, the shi-ning shore We may almost dis - cov - er.

2 We'll gird our loins, my brethren dear,
   Our distant home discerning;
Our absent Lord has left us word,
   Let every lamp be burning—
        For oh! &c.

3 Should coming days be cold and dark,
   We need not cease our singing;
That perfect rest nought can molest,
   Where golden harps are ringing.
        For oh! &c.

4 Let sorrow's rudest tempest blow,
   Each cord on earth to sever,
Our King says, come, and there's our home,
   For ever, oh! for ever!
      For oh! &c.

HAPPY DAY.

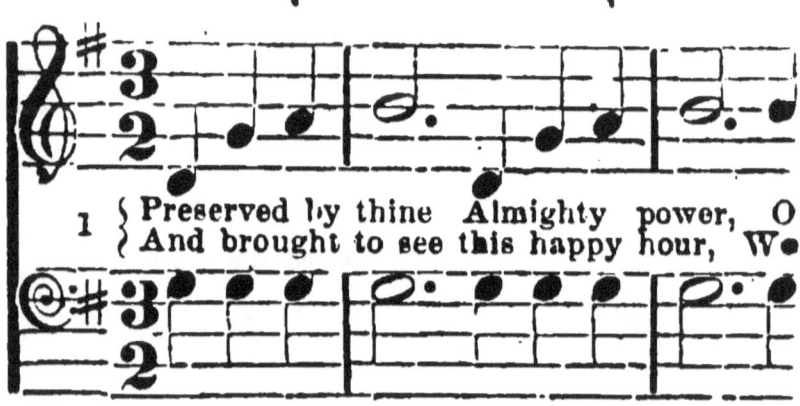

1 { Preserved by thine Almighty power, O
    { And brought to see this happy hour, We

S Chorus.

{ Lord   our   Maker, . Saviour,   King, } Happy
{ come   thy   praises   here   to   sing. } Happy

day, Happy day, Here in thy courts we'll glad.
day, Happy day, When Christ shall wash our sins

End.

ly stay, And at 'thy footstool humbly
a - way.

End with 2d strain. S

pray. That thou wouldst take our sins away.

2 We praise thee for thy constant care,
    For life preserved, for mercies given ;
  Oh, may we still those mercies share,
    And taste the joys of sins forgiven.

Chorus :
        Happy day, happy day,
    Here in thy courts we'll gladly stay;
        Happy day, happy day,
    When Christ shall wash our sins away.

3 We praise thee for the joyful news
    Of pardon through a Saviour's blood ;
  Oh Lord, incline our hearts to choose
    The road to happiness and God.

Chorus :
        Happy day, happy day,
    Here in thy courts we'll gladly stay:
        Happy day, happy day,
    When Christ shall wash our sins away.

4 And when on earth our days are done,
    Grant, Lord, that we at length may join,
  Teachers and scholars round thy throne,
    The song of Moses and the Lamb.

Chorus :
        Happy day, happy day,
    Here in thy courts we'll gladly stay;
        Happy day, happy day,
    When Christ shall wash our sins away.

In the christian's home in glory, There remains a land of rest, There my Saviour's gone before me. To fulfil my soul's request; there is rest for the weary There

is rest for the weary, There is rest for the weary,

There is rest for you—On the other side of

Jordan, in the sweet delds of Eden, Where the tree of

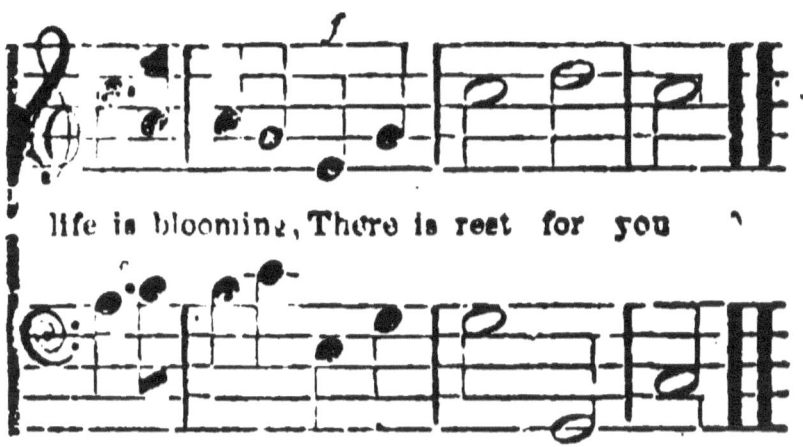

life is blooming, There is rest for you

2 He is fitting up my mansion,
   Which eternally shall stand;
For my stay shall not be transient,
   In that holy happy land.
      There is rest, &c.

3 Pain and sickness ne'er shall enter,
   Grief nor woe my lot shall share;
But in that celestial centre,
   I a crown of life shall wear.
      There is rest, &c.

4 Sing, O, sing ye heirs of glory,
   Shout your triumphs as you go;
Zion's gates will open for you,
   You shall find an entrance thro'.
      There is rest, &c.

I was a wandering sheep, I did not love

the fold ; I did not love my Father's voice, I would

not be controlled ; I was a wayward child, I

did not love my home, I did not love my Shepherd's voice, I loved afar to roam.

2 The Shepherd sought the sheep,
   The Father sought his child;
They followed me o'er vale and hill,
   O'er deserts waste and wild;
They found me nigh to death,
   Famished, and faint, and lone;
They bound me with the bands of love,
   They saved the wandering one.

No more a wandering sheep;
  I love to be controlled,
I love my tender shepherd's voice,
  I love the peaceful fold;
No more a wayward child,
  I seek no more to roam,
·I love my heavenly Father's voice,
  I love, I love his home.

S. M.

A CHARGE to keep I have,
  A God to glorify;
A never-dying soul to save,
  And fit it for the sky.
To serve the present age,
  My calling to fulfil;
O may it all my powers engage,
  To do my master's will.

2 Arm me with jealous care,
  As in thy sight to live;
And, O thy servant, Lord, prepare,
  A strict account to give.
Help me to watch and pray,
  And on thyself rely;
Assured, if I my trust betray
  I shall for ever die.

Say, brothers, will you meet us? Say, brothers, &c.
Say, Sisters, will you meet us? Say, sisters, &c.

meet us? Say, brothers, will you &c. On Canaan's
meet us? Say, sisters, will you &c. On Canaan's

happy shore!
happy shore!

2 By the grace of God we'll meet you.
   Where parting is no more;
   That will be a happy meeting,
   On Canaan's happy shore.

3 Jesus lives, and reigns forever,
   On Canaan's happy shore;
   Glory! glory! hallelujah!
   Forever, ever more.

INDEX OF TUNES.

FOR INDEX OF HYMNS, SEE PAGE 72.